WITHDRAWN

Ghostly Tales of Route 66:
Arizona to California

By Connie (Corcoran) Wilson, M.S.

Dedication

This book is dedicated to all the friendly and helpful folks along Route 66 who helped me so much, by sharing their stories and, in some cases, their hospitality. The list is too long to mention each of you by name (although some of their pictures appear in Volumes II and III), but please know that I will be eternally grateful.

I especially want to thank Rick Clark of Nashville and Santa Monica for the use of his shots of Santa Monica's Pier. Thanks, Rick!

Connie (Corcoran) Wilson, M.S.

© 2010 Connie Corcoran Wilson

All rights reserved. No part of this book may be reproduced or transmitted in any form or by any means, electronic or mechanical, including photocopying, recording, or by any informational storage or retrieval system, except by a reviewer who may quote brief passages in a review to be printed in a magazine or newspaper without permission in writing from the publisher.

The reader should understand that we were able to obtain some of these stories only if we promised to obscure the actual identity of persons and/or property. This required us to occasionally use fictitious names. In such cases, the names of the people and/or the places are not to be confused with actual places or actual persons living or dead.

TABLE OF CONTENTS

Four from Flagstaff	13
Wraiths of the Riordan Mansion	14
Monte Vista's Morbid Moments	35
The Weatherford at the Witching Hour	45
The Museum Club at Midnight	53
Jerome, Arizona	61
Williams, Arizona	65
The Spirits of Seligman	81
Kingman, Arizona	93
Oatman, Arizona: Tribute to a Kidnapped Girl	107
"Go West, Young Man!"	115
Suicide Bridge, Pasadena, California	130

Dinosaurs...or replicas of them...along Route 66.

Four From Flagstaff

Four from Flagstaff refers both to the four friends who set off on a grand ghost-hunting adventure as their senior year in college at Northern Arizona University commenced, and to the four Flagstaff haunted sites that initiated their road trip from Arizona to California. They would travel the Mother Road before their senior year of college in the dog days of summer, and investigate ghostly stories and sites along the way.

The four friends were Sidney Sheldon, Shelly Carlton, Laura Klinkenberg and Bob Hooper, all seniors at Northern Arizona University in Flagstaff, Arizona. They had been friends from grade school through high school and had gone on to attend the university in their mutual hometown of Flagstaff, Arizona.

Experience the sights and sounds of the stretch of Route 66 between Arizona and through California to the Pacific Ocean with the four from Flagstaff.

Riordan Mansion, 409 Riordan Road, Flagstaff, Arizona.

Wraiths of the Riordan Mansion

Sidney had always been the fussy one. If he were compared to a character on a TV show, it would be Sheldon of television's "The Big Bang Theory." Some people speculate that Sheldon suffers from Aspberger's Syndrome, a high-functioning version of autism. The four of us had been classmates since kindergarten, which is a long time, since we were now students entering our senior fall semester at Northern Arizona University, a school of roughly 20,000.

"How many kids can say that they went all the way through elementary school, junior high school, high school and college together?" Shelly used to ask the group. She was often Sheldon's spokesperson and self-appointed protector, since they were neighbors. Shelly was the pretty popular one. She had always been able to date anyone she wanted, it seemed. Not so much the case with me. I'm an acquired taste.

Sidney was an Art History major, and he was deeply in to various periods of furniture. If we had to hear one more word about Gustav Stickley, world famous furniture designer, I thought I would scream.

Sidney wanted his good friends Shelly, Bob and me, Laura, to go through the spooky Riordan Mansion at 409 Riordan Road, right across Riordan Road from Northern Arizona University. We even went over there as a foursome once, but the curators wouldn't let us go through the house unless we paid six dollars apiece, which none of us had, at the time. Plus, it's a "hands off" type tour with no picture taking allowed.

"Never mind," Shelly told the docent. "We'll come back later."

And coming back later is what we were doing now…coming back at close to midnight. Some might say we were breaking into the historic old mansion built by Dennis Matthew Riordan in 1884, but I prefer to think of it as liberating the treasures of the house for public view. After all, what good is a tour where you can't touch anything? Getting Bob to go along with this plan was difficult.

"I'm a business major," said Bob. "What do I want to be doing breaking into a spooky old log house?" Bob was a former high school quarterback and very good-looking. He was definitely too good-looking for our foursome, with the possible exception of Shelly. I suspected he had a thing for her and always would have.

"It's not a log house," Shelly said, sounding exasperated and dodging Bob's main point. "It's actually a frame house. They just put left-over ponderosa pine slabs from the mill on the outside, over the frame."

"Whatever," answered Bob, snubbing out a cigarette he wasn't supposed to be smoking. No smoking within 150 feet of the college's main entrance. "I've only got three classes to go and I'm out of here for good," Bob continued. "My life as an adult will officially commence. I'll be out of you three losers' lives, once and for all."

I thought that Shelly looked a bit crestfallen when Bob said that. Bob, of course, was smiling as he delivered the line, but sometimes Bob was oblivious to his effect on others. *Not unlike Sidney*, I thought.

"Nice, Bob. Really nice," said Sidney, also noticing Shelly's silent scowl. He smoothed the rumpled cover of his notebook, coming off as the prissy maiden aunt, smoothing her crocheted doilies. Sidney mounted his soapbox. "I just think that getting a little culture into your boring life might broaden your horizons somewhat. After you graduate, what? Are you going to live in a trailer and sit around in a tee shirt drinking Pabst Blue Ribbon and watching sports on TV?"

"Yeah, probably," said Bob. "Except for the trailer part. With a business degree and a computer science minor, I'll actually be able to get a job, instead of graduating with a useless degree in Art History like you'll have, Sidney. You'll probably have to move back home with your parents and learn to say, 'Would you like fries with that?'" Bob smiled.

I leaped to Sidney's defense. "We can't all be computer geeks like you, Bob. Sidney may be the next Gustav Stickley." I didn't really want to use Stickley in my sentence, but, honestly, since I'm an English major, he was the only furniture designer I knew.

"Never! I will never move back home with my parents," said Sidney indignantly. "My parents would never allow that."

I don't know if this was supposed to be a joke, but it certainly made me smile. Bob laughed outright. Sidney smoothed a wrinkle from his corduroy pants, the kind of slacks that nobody had worn since the seventies. Shelly just looked concerned.

"Well, then, what are you planning on doing with this wonderful Art History degree?" Bob asked Sidney. As he asked, Bob gave Sidney a genuinely inquisitive look. Shelly and I were also interested in hearing Sidney's response.

"If you must know, I'm thinking of becoming an architect like Frank Lloyd Wright. And, as most of you probably *don't* know, Wright often designed the furniture to go into his homes. I want to do the whole thing: the house, the furniture, the landscaping."

"Ooooh, Sidney Lloyd Wright II," I laughed. But what Sidney said made sense.

Sidney was smarter than all three of us combined, and he could become whatever he wanted to become. The only thing holding him back was his lack of social skills. To work designing buildings or furniture, he wouldn't need people skills. Perfect!

Sidney continued. "We've been across the street from this architectural treasure for almost four years and yet we have never been inside it, except for the main floor visitors' lobby that time we realized we didn't have twenty-four dollars amongst us, which was kind of sad, if you think about it. Did you know that there is one room where everything in the house is designed in an oval pattern? They've assembled most of the original furniture, too. One room has a canoe-shaped dining room table specially commissioned by the three Riordan brothers. Timothy and Michael Riordan, lumber barons, married the two Metz sisters, Caroline and Elizabeth."

"Wow! You really know a lot about this house, then, Sidney. And you're on a first-name basis with the dead sisters, too. Why didn't you apply for a job giving tours while you were in college? It's right across the street from school?"

Sidney looked uncomfortable. "Well, actually, I did, but they didn't hire me."

"Gee, " I said. "I can't imagine why. And you're so good with people, too!" My sarcasm must have been obvious.

Everyone laughed except Sidney, who looked distraught.

"So, are you three going to accompany me tonight on a little unscheduled tour of the house, or are you put off by the five acres of ponderosa pines that surround the place, which we'll have to sneak through to gain access without getting caught?"

"Have you taken a good look at the place?" asked Shelly. "It's creepy as hell! It looks like that hotel in 'The Shining.'"

"That would be 'The Overlook' in Colorado," said Sidney in his normal pedantic manner. "And it actually looks nothing like it. If you want to see a place that reminds of 'The Overlook,' I'll take you all downtown to the Monte Vista Hotel. Now *that* lobby looks like a tiny version of 'The Overlook' This is our last year in college, and I have several landmark structures that I want to expose you know-nothings to before you graduate and I never see you again. In fact, if this goes well and we get away with it, we might wish to consider a road trip before our senior year starts in two weeks."

"Oh, Sidney, honey. Getting rid of us isn't going to be *that* easy," I said. Shelly laughed, at least, finally realizing that we were kidding around.

"So, when are we going to do this daring deed?" asked Bob, preparing to head for the parking lot and home.

"Tonight. Near midnight. We park our cars here in the University lot and walk across Riordan Road and gather behind that stand of Ponderosa pines you can see from here." Sidney seemed to have thought of everything.

"Okay, Sherlock," I said. "I'll be here. How about the rest of you cretins?"

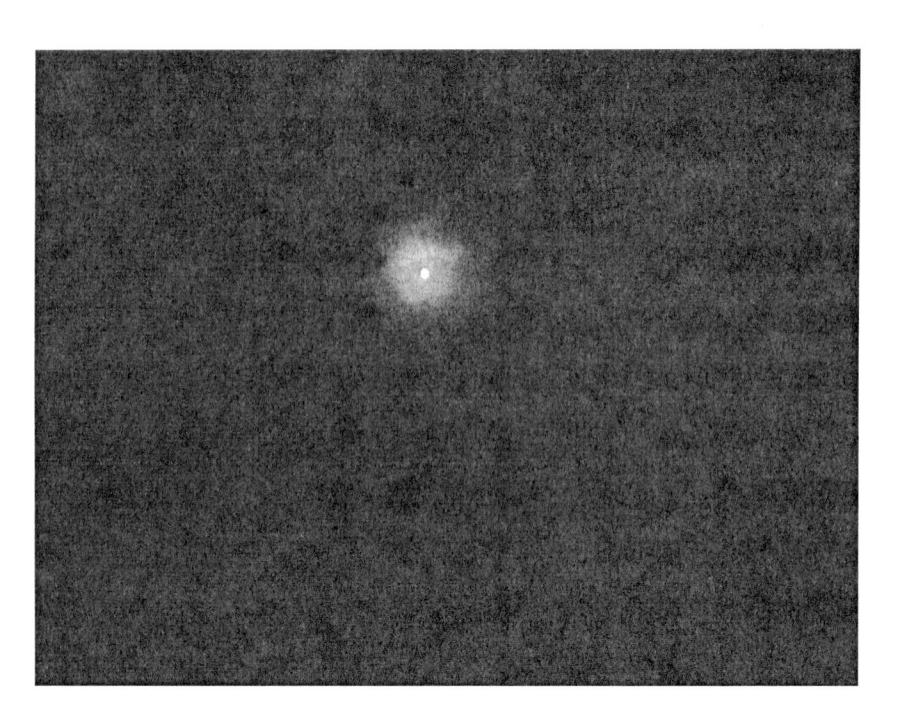

Shelly seemed hesitant, but said, "Well, if Sidney really wants to tour the place and knows what we'll be looking at, I'm in, but we can't break anything or hurt the house or its contents."

"Hurt the house?" said Sidney. He sounded offended. "The place is a masterpiece! I wouldn't dream of disturbing it. I just want to study it. Did you know that it has forty rooms…not counting the basement?"

"We don't have to go down to the basement, do we?" asked Shelly. It was a very girl-y comment.

Sidney responded with details, as he always did. "Our main thrust will be to see the 13,000 square feet of the residence. The brothers built two 6,000-foot homes that were just alike and then had them joined together by a 1,000 square foot common room known as 'the cabin.' Isn't that cool? Charles Whittlesey, who designed the El Tovar Hotel of the Grand Canyon, designed the entire structure. It has some wonderful Harvey Ellis-designed inlay furniture. And, of course, the 1904 Gustav Stickley furniture...."

"Not Stickley AGAIN," I moaned. "Please, just stop with the Stickley stuff." I stuffed a piece of sugarless gum in my mouth and began chomping noisily. *There's another furniture designer name for next time I need one in a trivia competition: Harvey Ellis.*

"I'll not mention Stickley or his furniture again if YOU promise to quit chewing your gum like a cow chewing its cud," Sidney said. He sniffed disapprovingly and then turned to his oldest friend and childhood playmate. "Shelly, are you ready to depart?" Only Sidney would say depart instead of leave. This was Sidney's way of letting us know that we could all go home for dinner. It was close to 6 p.m. and the staff at the Riordan Mansion, which ended its tours at 5:30 p.m., could be seen leaving in their cars. We were done registering for our senior year of college, and adventure seemed to beckon just beyond the horizon.

"But how are we going to get in the house?" asked Bob, always the practical one.

"Leave that to me," said Sidney, "but all of you must bring a flashlight or torch of some sort, so that we can find our way around without turning on any electricity. We don't want to get arrested for breaking and entering. We won't *really* be breaking and entering, anyway."

"What do you mean? We'll be entering a locked house after it is closed for tours of the day. How are we not breaking and entering?" I asked.

"When I interviewed for that docent position, it just so happened that I came into possession of a key to the back door," said Sidney. He looked evasive and didn't meet the group's interested gaze.'

"How? Why?" I asked. Shelley and Bob were also interested in what Sidney was going to answer.

Sidney sniffed. "Let's just say that, when they refused to consider hiring me as a docent because of my…. my condition…(Sidney always hated to refer to his Aspberger's Syndrome by its official title), I threw a little bit of a hissy-fit and the caretaker went to get me a Diet Coke. While she was gone, I noticed a key near the door on a table, and I happened to pick it up. I forgot that I had put it in my pocket when I left."

Bob snorted openly. "You 'forgot' that you stole a key?" He seemed genuinely amused by Sidney's explanation.

So it was that the four of us---Sidney, me, Shelly and Bob---all gathered at Kinlichi Knoll under a stand of Ponderosa pine trees that stood near the back door of the large mansion. If you're not a local, it's really difficult to tell if you're in the front or the back of the house, anyway, but this was supposed to be the back of the place. I nearly fell down stumbling over what looked like an old wagon wheel standing near the sidewalk leading to the back door. Everything about the house was gloomy and reminded of redwood trees, or, more accurately, Ponderosa pine trees.

Sidney slid the key in the door; it creaked open noisily, and we tiptoed silently into the main floor visitors' center area, our flashlights lighting the way.

"You see," said Sidney, our unofficial guide," the two Riordan brothers, Timothy and Michael, built two identical houses which were then connected by the common area room I told you about, where the two families would meet and often play billiards and other games. They also built a mini-chapel on the second floor."

"Tell me again why we didn't just bring our six bucks and take the tour during the day, because this place is seriously giving me the creeps, " I said.

Sidney made it a point to answer. "We didn't take the tour not only because of the money—which we didn't have—but also because they wouldn't let us take pictures or touch anything, Silly. Remember?"

"No, actually, I don't remember. I remember being quite happy that I wasn't going to have to spend very much time inside this scary place." Just then a floorboard creaked. I let out an involuntary cry.

"Keep it down to a low roar," Bob said, laughing at my nervousness.

We were now in the common area room about three feet from the billiard table. I watched as the eight ball was hit towards the side pocket and dropped. A dartboard also hung on a far wall. The unmistakable sound of a dart hitting the target could be heard, although not seen in the twilight of our flashlight's brilliance.

"Who did that?" I asked knowing that nobody was going to answer me.

"Perhaps I should have told you that this room is reputed to be haunted,' Sidney said.

"WHAT?" Shelley shrieked.

"Timothy's oldest daughter, Anna, and Michael's son, Arthur, both died of polio within hours of one another in 1927. They held the funeral right here in this room."

Now there was a bit of news that did nothing to reassure me.

"It was very sad," said Sidney. "Elizabeth, Michael's wife, nursed her adult daughter Anna throughout her illness. Anna was only twenty-six and engaged to be married at the time. Really a sad thing, especially since it was probably from Anna that Arthur contracted the disease. It was highly contagious, you know. There wasn't a cure until Jonas Salk came up with the polio vaccine in the fifties. It did cause some friction between the brothers, but the families gathered together in this very room with just the minister and immediate family members present to hold the service and send Anna and Arthur off to their great reward."

"And what great reward was that?" Bob asked. We'd all known each other for so long that the three of us were well aware that Bob, an atheist, believed that all you got after death was a dirt nap. The Big Sleep.

"Well, let's try to concentrate on the glories of the room, shall we?" said Sidney, turning the conversation away from religious differences amongst the group.

"The house was built in 1904 and sits on six acres of woodland. Volcanic stone arches. Hand-split wooden shingles. It has many modern conveniences that we take for granted today, but which the Riordans engineered earlier. It's really an architectural marvel, and it is my self-appointed duty to fill you know-nothings in on some of the architectural jewels of our fair city of Flagstaff and beyond before we all graduate and go our separate ways. Consider this our first adventure."

Just then we heard a tremendous crash from upstairs. We all looked uneasily at one other. I said, "And maybe our last adventure? What was that?"

"Yes, what was that?" Shelly asked. Her eyes in the flashlight's glare glowed red like a cornered squirrel.

"That? Well, that could have been any of a number of things," said Sidney. "Let's go upstairs and find out, shall we?"

There was no enthusiasm for this course of action, but we reluctantly followed the oblivious Sidney to the upper second floor, where large dress dummies, one clad in a lavender dress of the late 1800's stood.

Another of the dummies, clad in a white dress that looked as though it might have been Anna's wedding dress---the one she never got to wear---had fallen towards a green wicker porch chair suspended on chains. The dummy had not crashed all the way to the floor because its descent was stopped by the suspended swing.

"Why would they have a swing chair like that in an upstairs bedroom?" asked Shelly.

"Probably it was somewhere else, originally, but the curator wants to preserve all the original furniture and things like the dresses the Riordan women wore, as well, and, because they charge for the tour, they may have moved the porch swing upstairs."

"Hideous kinky," said Bob, ignoring the fact that Shelly and I were terrified.

Just then, we heard a clicking sound from down below in the common area room. It was the sound of a billiard game in progress. We raced back downstairs and watched for five minutes as various balls on the billiard table rolled towards (and, in most cases dropped into) various pockets.

Bob said, "My advice is not to stand in the line of fire of that dartboard target behind you, Shelly." Shelly had, indeed, been standing right in the line of fire. We could still see the red feathers of the last dart embedded in the bulls' eye of the target glistening in our flashlight beams. Shelly moved as quickly as the cornered squirrel her eyes had begun to resemble, to scamper to safety.

"I don't know about you guys," I said, "but I think I've seen enough Gustav Stickler furniture, and I don't give a fig for that inlay guy. I just want to get out of here."

My vote for leaving the haunted house was accompanied by what appeared to be a young woman drifting across the top of the staircase, her feet a good three feet above the floor. It was the same staircase we had just descended and the dress appeared to be the same lavender dress that had been displayed on the fallen dummy when we visited the upstairs bedroom of Anna Riordan.

"The lavender lady..." breathed Shelly.

"You've got that wrong," I said. "The lavender lady haunts the Lemp Mansion in St. Louis."

Then, we heard the sound of footsteps on the roof.

Even Sidney was alarmed, thinking it might be night security officers. We exited the building, carefully locking it behind us, and sprinted for our cars in the Northern Arizona University parking lot across the street.

"Thanks, again, Sidney, for a memorable evening," Bob said. "I'm happy to report that none of us was killed by whatever was in that house." Bob's hands shook as he lit another of his omnipresent cigarettes.

"You're welcome, Bob," Sidney answered, ignoring or missing the irony in Bob's voice.

"Tomorrow, then, for our next architectural ramble?" Sidney was really amazing. He seemed rather calm…considering. I didn't feel like going through the spooky Riordan Mansion again and said so.

"Oh, I don't mean the Riordan Mansion. Tomorrow night I'm taking you lot on a tour of a downtown hotel."

"What hotel?" asked Shelly. "And why?"

"Well, it's a really neat place, the Monte Vista Hotel. Your crack about the 'Overlook' made me realize that you three probably have never been inside what is a city-owned jewel of a hotel. Plus, it has some interesting history. Some say it's haunted. Tomorrow, then? Unless the Riordan Mansion ghosts come after us," Sidney said.

Somehow, Sidney's little joke did not bring smiles to our faces as we finished off the night's big adventure. But he had secured a promise from us that we would meet at the Monte Vista Hotel at 100 N. San Francisco Street in the downtown area at 7:00 p.m. the very next night.

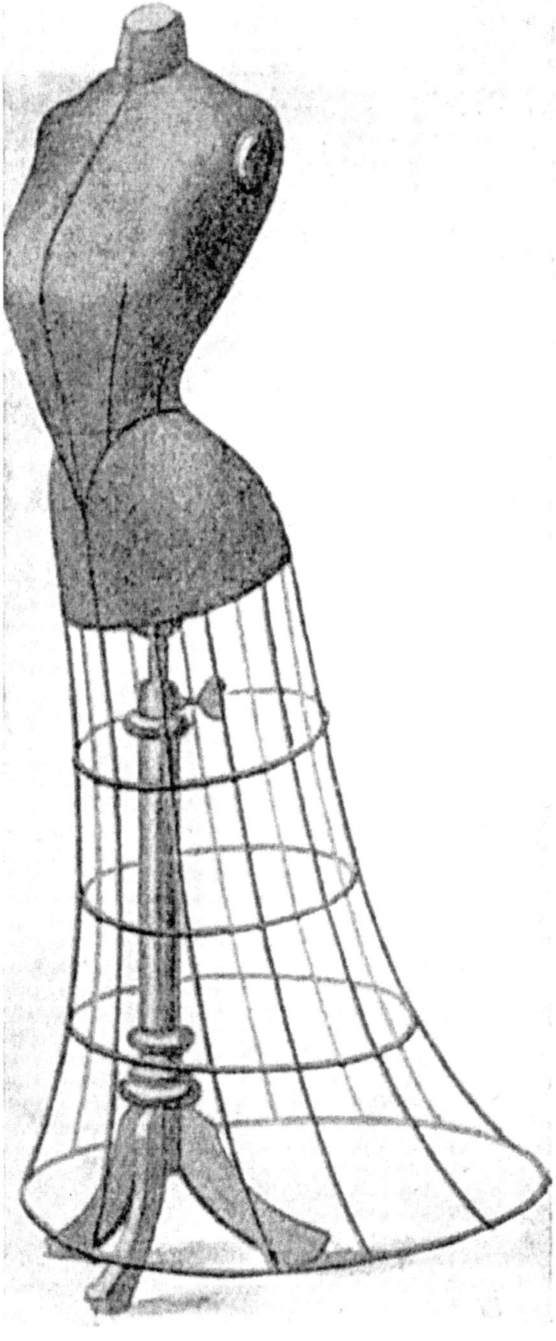

Monte Vista Hotel, Flagstaff, Arizona

Monte Vista Hotel, Flagstaff, Arizona

The very next night, we all gathered in the downtown area of Flagstaff, Arizona. I noticed that the outside of the Monte Vista Hotel at 100 N. San Francisco Street (circa 1927, said the metal plaque) had some interesting balconies outside the rooms. I kept shooting digital pictures of the balconies, more because I thought it would impress Sidney that I was noticing the architecture than for any other reason. I was just drawn towards them. I also took pictures of the sign on the side of the hotel, of the entrance, and of the door to the basement.

It wasn't until later that I learned that some local outlaws holed up in the Gary Cooper room, as it is known, which had balconies, and summoned ladies of the evening. After over-imbibing, the outlaws threw the girls from the balconies to their deaths in the street below.

"Wow! Yet another spooky, creepy midnight rendezvous. Is it possible for the four of us to do something normal, like go to a movie?" asked Shelley.

"Why would you want to sit in a boring movie, probably based on a children's toy or something equally juvenile, when we're young adults about to graduate from college and begin our real lives?" Sidney seemed sincere.

"Never mind, Sidney," said Shelly. "You wouldn't understand."

I said, "Uh...because it's safer to go to the movies?" Sidney ignored me.

We entered the weathered-looking old-fashioned hotel. It did resemble a smaller version of the Outlook Hotel. There was a plaque on the inside wall as you entered that paid tribute to the fact that this hotel was the longest publicly held commercial hotel in America. V.M. Slipher, in 1924, decided the city should pass an ordinance establishing a municipal bond to build it.

Back when they filmed westerns in nearby Sedona and Oat Creek Canyon, the movie stars of that day were frequently housed in Flagstaff, as Sedona had not yet grown into the tourist destination it is today. Rooms are named after famous stars and one of the rooms of the hotel was actually used in the filming of the movie "Casablanca." Among the famous rooms supposed to be haunted are the Zane Grey Room (#210), which has a bell-boy who knocks and disappears, room number twenty, which once housed an eccentric who hung raw meat from the chandelier, and room number 305, where a female ghost of the establishment is often seen rocking in a rocking chair.

MONTE VISTA HOTEL
100 N. SAN FRANCISCO
CIRCA 1927

As I was reading the plaque devoted to the fact that the community had pitched in to build the hotel, I noticed another plaque inside that drew me to it just as surely as a compass needle points to magnetic north. I took several pictures of a metal plaque that proclaimed this was the door to the basement of the hotel. I had no idea that there was a legend that had circulated for years about a famous movie star, housed in the hotel during the shooting of a film in Sedona, who kept hearing the sound of a small child crying. The crying seemed to be coming from the basement. This kind-hearted actor---I'll call him Marion Morrison---descended to the basement and took the hand of the small boy he found there.

"Come on, Son," he said to the small child. "Let's find your mother." And the actor climbed back up to the main floor, the boy climbing the stairs, following behind him. But, when Marion reached the top step of the basement stairs near the lobby desk and looked behind him, there was no one there.

One room of the hotel has been permanently locked and is not rented to travelers. The reason? Phone calls come in at all hours of the day and night, and a phantom bus boy is often reported to be incessantly knocking at the door. It's said that the entire floor is subject to ghosts who roam and whisper. All who have stayed in one of the hotel's room have reported being constantly disturbed, so much so that the hotel finally made the place off limits, especially to travelers with pets, as dogs and cats go berserk in the room.

Here we were, the Four Musketeers, all dressed up with some place to go. And that place was very likely haunted!

Sidney assumed his usual role as Mr. Know-It-All of 2010. "Did any of you notice when this hotel was built, from the plaque outside?" asked our friend.

Bob replied, "It said, 'Circa 1927.'"

"Good, Bob. Good for you," said Sidney, like the little professor he resembled in real life. "In actuality, this hotel was officially opened on New Year's Day of 1927. Since that time many famous movie stars have stayed here, including Gary Cooper, Spencer Tracy, Jane Russell, John Wayne and Bing Crosby."

I waited for Bob to make a bad joke involving Jane Russell's most obvious physical attributes, but Bob seemed genuinely interested in what Sidney was going to say next.

The lobby of the Monte Vista Hotel in downtown Flagstaff, Arizona.

Sidney continued, "To the left you see the entrance to the Monte Vista Lounge, which, in 1930 and 1931, was *the* place to be seen in Flagstaff. They even had slot machines in here for a while. But the weirdest story about the Monte Vista Lounge took place in the 1970's after a bank robbery."

The Monte Vista Bank nearby was robbed. There were three gunmen. They pulled a daring robbery. After they had grabbed the cash, police pursued them. Shots were fired. The three abandoned their getaway car…"

"What kind of car was it?" Bob interrupted him.

Sidney, who had no interest in cars, unlike most boys his age, brushed the question aside saying, "I don't know. A red car," and, without even breaking stride continued, "and fled here, to the Monte Vista Lounge. The robbers' plan was to stay here until the cops gave up and left the area. They'd stay in the bar until the cops left the area. They sat in that booth right over there, the semi-circular one."

I'd done a little reading of my own, so I spoke up.

"The abandoned get-away car," I said, "was a 1969 Chevrolet Camaro Z-28. Those cars came with a 302 cubic inch V8 engine with factory-advertised horsepower ratings of 290 with the single four-barrel carburetor. They were built solely to allow General Motors to compete in the TransAm racing class, where there was a five-liter (305 cubic inch) limit on engine size. They were only available with a four-speed manual transmission, but there were a myriad of options, once they were available, to be ordered by the public. "

"Wow!" remarked Bob. "Laura knows cars. Who knew?"

By now, we were all curious. We had all moved to the door of the lounge to gawk.

Type of getaway car the robbers abandoned.

"Since they were fleeing the law, the robbers were trying not to attract attention, so they ordered drinks. One of the bank robbers had been hit in the fuselage of bullets, though, and---despite his friends' attempts to staunch the flow of blood from his wounds---he died before he finished his first drink. Right in that booth."

"Talk about your Bloody Mary's," cracked Bob. "Maybe they should name a drink in his honor. They could call it the Bloody Larry."

"Bob---that's not funny. A man died right over there," said Shelly, pointing at the booth with horror.

"That's not the worst of it," continued Sidney. "Many of the bar's patrons claim that, if they move to that booth, fresh wet blood stains appear on the cocktail napkins and on the floor beneath the booth. After closing, the help says that they hear drink glasses clinking from over in that booth, when there's nobody in the place except them. They haven't seen any of the robbers in here…yet…but there are plenty of sightings elsewhere in this hotel."

"What do you mean?" asked Shelly, seemingly hypnotized by Sidney's dramatic delivery of this story.

"Well, even today many of the hotel's residents are from Europe. In fact, 50% of its current clientele come to stay in the themed rooms, which rent today for seventy-five to ninety-five bucks a night. But, back then, this was a luxury hotel, and one particular luxury movie star who died of cancer after filming on what was a former missile test range…and she was one of the biggest…once won an Oscar playing a woman condemned to death in the gas chamber…that movie star is sometimes seen walking right through the door into the hotel room she stayed in. There's talk that, if you are in the women's bathroom, she appears in the mirror behind you. Stuff like that."

This last bit of wisdom sent me scurrying to the rest room area, where I found a very lavish, ornately framed bathroom mirror. I even took a picture of it, but I saw no movie star ghosts appearing alongside my reflection.

"I don't care what you say, Sidney," said Shelly." I'm NOT going to the basement. So, where's our next adventure to be?"

"Let's sit down in that booth over there," (indicating the corner booth just discussed) "order a quick drink, and then we'll walk down to the Weatherford Hotel, the next corner down. Then, this weekend, be sure to save Saturday night. We're going to the Museum Club, and that place is always jumping on the weekend."

"How would you know, Sidney?" Bob asked wryly. He had taken a Pall Mall from his pack of cigarettes. He was about to light up.

"You'd be surprised at the wealth of knowledge that a person can acquire through reading, Bob. You ought to try it some time."

Touché, Sidney, I thought.

"So, we're on for the Weatherford Hotel one block north of the Mother Road next, and then, on the weekend, we do the Museum Club?"

"Exactly, Laura. And thanks so much for listening." Sidney headed towards the haunted booth, with the three of us reluctantly following the little professor in our midst.

The Weatherford Hotel Lobby.

44

The Weatherford at the Witching Hour

We spent so much time exploring the Monte Vista that it was nearly midnight when we walked the two blocks to the Weatherford Hotel, another fine Flagstaff establishment located at 23 N. Leroux Street (928-779-1919).

Established in 1900 on New Year's Day by John Weatherford, many famous people have stayed in the hotel, including William Randolph Hearst, Teddy Roosevelt, western author Zane Grey (for whom the ballroom is now named), Wyatt Earp and water colorist Thomas Moran.

Sidney began, standing on the steps leading to the hotel's upper floor rooms, "John Weatherford also built the Majestic Opera

House in 1911, but it burned down in 1915. Undeterred, Weatherford rebuilt the opera house, this time naming it the Orpheum.

This hotel has been home to many businesses, including the first telephone company, various restaurants, a theater, a radio station, and a billiard parlor."

Just then a loud train whistle, sounding more forlorn than usual in the midnight darkness, echoed throughout the building.

Flagstaff, Arizona Train Depot, Now the Visitors' Center

There isn't a single thirty-minute stretch of time that a train doesn't come rolling through just two blocks away in downtown Flagstaff, so ear plugs are often offered to guests of the Weatherford. The décor of the individual guest rooms can best be described as gloomy and antiquated.

The lobby, however, has a cozy feeling, with a carpeted room as you enter, a staircase ascending to the back, the Zane Grey Ballroom with its stained glass windows and an antique Brunswick bar brought from Tombstone. Straight ahead and to the left as you enter, a cozy restaurant with a fireplace and tables. The nightlife in downtown Flagstaff, which both the Monte Vista Hotel and the Weatherford are located right in the middle of, is supposed to roar on until 2:30 a.m. or later, with fellow students from the 20,000 student campus helping swell the ranks of revelers. The local police respond to any and all calls with sirens blaring.

"Let's head into the Ballroom," Bob said to the three of us. We could hear a band playing in that general vicinity, but, when we entered, there was no band in sight. There was, however, a billiards table, and a light above it, which is reported to sway back and forth with no explanation for this movement. A female form sometimes is reported floating above the ballroom floor, or darting from side to side.

There is another bar on the third floor, and we went there for four-dollar drinks and two-dollar beers. There, a band really was playing.

Sidney began, "When the Majestic Opera House was built in 1911, it was the pride of the town. However, it burned down in 1915, and, supposedly at least one person was killed in the blaze. That person is said to haunt the current Orpheum. That's the name of the place with which John Weatherford replaced the Majestic Opera House after the blaze. Also," continued Sidney, "just a couple blocks away there's the train station."

Weatherford Hotel Cafe

"Yes, we know," said Shelly sarcastically. "We live here. This is our home town."

"But did you know that it is supposed to be haunted by the ghost of a railroad man who was killed in the station house one night when a train jumped the tracks?"

"I didn't know that," I said, speaking up first. "Did you hear that from Justin?"

Justin Connors is one of the tour guides who assists visitors and leads tours at the old train station. He is also a native American.

"No, I didn't hear it from Justin," said Sidney. Sidney looked peeved. "I think I read it in the *Lumberjack*."

"You read it in our college newspaper?" I asked. "Why would they have an article about a ghost haunting the train station in our college newspaper?"

"To be honest, the *Lumberjack* had an article about it because I submitted it," said Sidney. He looked a bit perturbed to have to admit he had written the piece.

"Figures," said Bob.

"When are we all going to go hang at the Museum Club? I am definitely up for that." That would be Bob, of course.

"The Museum Club is Saturday night, which is tomorrow night. Be there or be square. Bring some money and a camera. You all know where it is, right?" asked Sidney.

"It's two and one-half miles east of downtown, on Route 66," I said. "See you all there tomorrow night at 7 p.m. Wear your dancing shoes."

"One small thing, Sidney," said Bob as we began walking towards his parked car.

"What?" asked Sidney.

"Nobody has said, 'Be there or be square' since, oh, 1950 or so."

I was still chuckling as I headed towards my own vehicle, parked near Bob's.

ROUTE 66 ROADSIDE ATTRACTION

MUSEUM CLUB, FLAGSTAFF, ARIZONA
Beneath the inverted, forked ponderosa entryway awaits an adventure in pioneer history, country-western legends and ghost stories - one of northern Arizona's liveliest landmarks since 1931.
Recognized by Hampton Hotels Save-A-Landmark program as a site worth seeing

The Museum Club at Midnight

The big electric neon guitar sign outside the Museum Club was lit up, proclaiming "Redneck: Live on Friday and Saturday Night!" "This place is sometime called 'the Zoo'" said Sidney. "Do you know why that is?"

'Because all the customers behave like animals?" Shelly asked, mock seriously.

"I know why," said Bob. "The original owner had a bunch of stuffed animals in the place. Weird stuff like six-legged sheep and two-headed calves."

"There were all kinds of displays, yes," said Sidney." Winchester rifles, Indian artifacts, stuffed animals of various sorts, over 30,000 artifacts collected by the original owner, Dean Eldredge of Wisconsin, who became interested in taxidermy when he found a petrified frog in Wisconsin."

"Shades of Jeffrey Dahmer," I murmured, under my breath.

Sidney continued, " By 1931, Mr. Eldredge had built this place to house his growing collection. When he died of cancer in 1936, much of his collection was sold off after ownership transferred to Doc Williams. The heyday of the place, however, --- its resurgence--- came about when Don 'Pappy' Scott bought the place in 1993.

Don was a musician and had played with some of the best in the land. His wife Thorna and he lived upstairs. Don used his connections with Nashville musicians to bring in country and western stars like Willie Nelson, Barbara Mandrell and Waylon Jennings. The dance floor was advertised as being the biggest wooden dance floor in the United States, or at least the biggest dance floor in Arizona. In fact, this place has been voted one of the Top Ten Roadhouses by *Car & Driver* magazine more than once. It's also on the National Register of Historic Places and is a readers' favorite dance club, as voted in a poll by *Country America* magazine."

"So, where do the ghosts come in?" I asked.

Sidney continued. "Don and Thorna, as I mentioned, lived above the front bar area. There is a pull-down staircase, like the kind that leads to attics. In 1973, Thorna tumbled down that staircase, breaking her neck. She lived for a brief period in a coma. When she died, Don was inconsolable. He was so grief-stricken that he took his own life. He shot himself with a rifle while seated in a rocking chair in front of the fireplace we will see as we enter. That was in 1975."

"Yikes!" said Shelly.

"Ever since then, the story is that the Museum Club is haunted by the ghosts of Don and Thorna Scott. We'll talk to some of the regulars and see what they have to say."

And with that, we entered the Museum Club.

As you enter, there are fireplaces with large wooden rocking chairs in front of them. I think we all wondered if one of the rocking chairs was the one Don 'Pappy' Scott had been sitting in when he shot himself. As if on cue, one of the rocking chairs began to gently move as we walked past it.

"Don't let that bother you, Folks," said a cheerful voice that turned out to belong to Jane Bliss, longtime bartender at the club. "It's just the wind coming in with you," she paused, "or a ghost." She was still smiling. We smiled back.

Jane has been a bartender at the Museum Club for almost ten years now. She gave us the tour, including the off-track betting parlor and the specific ponderosa pine (the dance floor is built around four of them) where a black man was shot and hanged by the locals. Jane pointed out how the tree---which stands in the middle of the dance floor---is singed. She called my attention to the many bullet holes in the tree itself. I sidled up next to the tree and whispered, "Barack Obama is now the President."

Off to the back left northwest corner of the room, behind the off-track betting parlor, which is in the front left-hand corner of the structure as you enter, is an old bar dating from the late 1800's. It is reportedly haunted. Many of the bar's employees have come in to work to find the figure of a woman behind the bar. When approached, she disappears. People have tried to order drinks from her, only to be told when they complain of the poor service that that bar is not open nor is it staffed. It is said that some have tried to buy the woman, sitting alone in the club, a drink. When they return, she has disappeared."

"That just sounds like some poor gal getting hit on by someone she doesn't want to have anything to do with," Shelly said. I smiled as Shelly made a big "L" with her thumb and fore-finger on her forehead as a silent comic comment.

A large scrapbook was produced. Old pictures of a bachelorette party in progress at the back bar were displayed. As the girls in the group—all pretty young things---began to dance atop the bar, orbs began to appear in the foreground of the photos taken of the girls atop the bar. First one orb, then two, then three, then multiple orbs. The employees believe that the ghosts of this haunted back bar were gathering to watch the beautiful young bride-to-be party at her bachelorette party. Orbs are believed to be a sign of ghostly phenomenon. I, myself, have taken at least one picture of orbs in a ghostly sighting at Fort El Reno, Oklahoma (p. 47, Volume II). The pictures in this Museum Club scrapbook, however, were dated and timed chronologically. Clearly the orbs were multiplying quickly as the party gathered steam.

Bob looked at them over my shoulder and commented, "They just look like dust bunnies, to me." Shelly snickered.

In 1978, Stacie and Martin Zanzucchi bought the bar. The ghost stories continued. Many of them center on the upstairs apartment where Don and Thorna Scott once resided. Lights turn on when no one lives there. One former renter of the space claimed that a female ghost actually jumped on him, held him down, and said, "You need only fear the living." He climbed out the window, running away from the apartment over the rooftop never to return.

"Did he send someone for his stuff?" asked Shelly.

"That's not the point," Sidney countered. "The young man was extremely traumatized by the encounter he had with something...or someone...in the apartment."

I spoke with the woman who runs the cage where the money is kept for the offtrack betting. Julie Ravera (not her real name) told me that she is often the first one to open the Museum Club, which opens at 11 a.m. and stays open until 2 a.m. No one but Julie has a key to the cage, since that is where the money is kept to pay off the betters. Yet she has observed a woman inside the cage and, when she approached the door, the door was unlocked, although she is the only one with a key and had not yet opened it for the day.

"One of the scariest things I ever experienced," said Julie," was the time I was here all by myself late at night, locking up, and I went into the rest room. No one else was here. The place had been closed for hours. I was inside one of the restroom stalls when I heard water running in one of the sinks. I called out, 'Is anybody there?' Nobody answered. When I came out of the stall, there was no one here, but the sink was overflowing and the water was still running."

Julie swears that she has seen a woman at the haunted back bar when no one else was in the building, and confirms that many hear footsteps walking upstairs---the apartment where Don and Thorna Scott lived---even though no one has rented the place for years.

"Well, I'm convinced," said Shelly, poring over the photos of the bachelorette party. "This place is really cool and woody and cozy, but I think it's haunted as hell. Let's get out of here."

" I hate to end our adventures, Kids. How about a road trip?" I said.

"Road trip where?" all three asked at once.

"We don't start school for almost two weeks. Why don't we take Route 66 to Williams and Seligman and Kingman and Oatman? Maybe even venture on as far as the coast? Who's with me?" I was beginning to feel a little bit like John Belushi in the classic scene from "Animal House."

All three smiled and Shelly said, "Great idea, Laura! We'll really make this a senior trip to remember."

"I'll figure out the itinerary and call each of you," I said. "First, I have to get a map and figure out the driving distance. But hold that thought."

Jerome, Arizona

We gathered to discuss our trip, and I got out a map.

"Whenever I mention 'ghosts' or 'haunted places,' everyone says the same thing: Jerome. If you look at this map, you can see that Jerome is due south of us here in Flagstaff, and not that far away, either. We really need to go see what Jerome is all about before we strike off for Williams, which is only thirty miles west of us. Any objections?"

Nobody said anything, so I continued, "There are two places in Jerome that we should visit. One is a place called the Haunted Hamburger, at 410 N. Clark Street. Eric and Michelle Jurisin own it now. They bought the place after it had been vacant for six years. It was the Wykoff Apartments in the 1920's."

"So, what's so unusual about this hamburger joint?" Sidney asked.

"As far as I can tell from my reading, there are the usual water on and off, lights on and off incidents and, when it was under renovation, hammers kept disappearing," I answered him.

"Ooooooo, the old disappearing hammer trick," Bob said, sarcastically.

"What about the hotel?" Shelly asked.

"We'll stay in the Connor Hotel, which has real ghostly promise," I answered. "It opened in 1898. Twenty-three rooms furnished with call bells, electricity and individual wood stoves. But it was pricey for its day, at one dollar a night. Now, however, it's pretty cheap. We should try to get the guys into room five or room one."

"Why those rooms, --- as if I didn't know," Sidney asked. He sighed. "And don't you mean ghastly promise?" We all smiled at Sidney's little joke.

"The usual, plus palm pilots and computers malfunction in those rooms."

"Oh, good. The only one of us who really cares about whether their computer works or not, and you assign me to a room where you *know* it won't work." Sidney sounded miffed.

"Let's move on from griping about losing our Twitter and Facebook connections and consider the history of the place," I said. "Dave Connor, its original owner, was farsighted enough to carry fire insurance in a day when few did. That was good, since the hotel burned down two times in two years. It reopened again in August of 1899."

"Do you think maybe the spirits were trying to tell Mr. Connor something by burning his hotel down twice in just two years?" asked Bob. Bob's sarcasm knew no bounds, but he *was* funny. "It doesn't sound like he was going to win the Good Housekeeping Seal of Approval."

"Maybe he was a closet pyromaniac," Sidney contributed, a serious look on his face.

"Enough with the speculation. If the powers-that-be were trying to tell Mr. Connor something, using fire, he was a spectacularly slow study, because he just kept rebuilding the hotel. Now we can experience whatever or whoever resides there from the spirit world. Usually, they are up to no good around two o'clock in the morning. In fact, they had a satellite television installer from Phoenix who ended up spending the night in his van when the ghosts wouldn't leave him alone. The second floor is supposed to be the worst. A niece of the owners said she heard a man's voice calling her name in the rest room on the second floor. She cleared out of there pretty quickly."

"No kidding," said Shelly. "I'd be ticked if a guy were in the women's rest room, whether he was whispering my name or not. I'd clear out, too!"

"Well, we're all in agreement, then? We'll make a slight detour to old haunted Jerome, spend the night, and then resume our drive to Williams?" No one objected.

Williams, Arizona

I drew up the schedule for the four of us to begin our road trip thirty miles to the west of Flagstaff, and the detour to Jerome did not change that plan. The weather was stifling and the old '57 Chevy wasn't air-conditioned. Since we were all twenty-one, there really wasn't much opposition from our parents to making the trip. They thought it was "quaint" that we were going to take a road trip across old Route 66, ending at the Santa Monica Pier. We took turns hanging our heads out the window like dogs because of the extreme heat.

"So, what do we know about Williams?" I was asking Sidney, who always seemed to be the one in the know, but Shelly and Bob were welcome to chime in.

Bob had borrowed his dad's '57 Chevy...a turquoise blue four-door with the classic fins. When we stopped to gas it up, I hopped out to help and couldn't find the gas tank. Apparently, they were concealed within the fin or something hinky. Bob found it very funny and set me up for that one.

"How much did this car set your dad back, Bob, when it was new, and why is he letting you have it for the trip?" I asked.

"Well, it's been in the family since 1957, when it cost around $3,000, I think. But Dad says it's worth $47,000 now. I don't know

Vintage '57 Chevy

if that's right or not, but he thought it would be cool if we traveled the Mother Road in a period car."

I interjected, "Someone I know who owned a two-door '57 convertible Chevy sold it for close to seventy-five thousand dollars just a year or so ago. He said that, if it had been fuel-injected, rather than the low horsepower dual quad engine in it, it would have gone for one hundred thousand. But, of course, that is if it is in excellent condition, which his was."

"What other hidden talents do you have, Laura, besides your knowledge of cars, hidden from all of us for so many years?" Bob asked, with a smile.

"Cool!" said Shelly. We were all getting into the spirit of the trip, but we were also sweating like we'd been abandoned in the desert or working on a chain gang for hours.

"We'll be in Williams before you know it. There's supposed to be a haunted walk of some sort that we can take part in tonight, if we want, led by the locals. Plus I've found us the perfect place to spend the night. It's only fifty-nine dollars and it's right in the heart of the downtown, across from the Chamber of Commerce and the train station area."

"Ooooo, I can hardly wait," said Bob. "Is it as good as the Connor Hotel?"

I gave Bob a withering look and prepared to continue.

"What's the name of the hotel?" asked Sidney.

"Appropriately enough, the Grand Canyon Hotel. The information online says it is the oldest operating hotel in the United States."

"You can't believe everything you read online," Bob said. "That hotel last night was as old as Methusaleh."

"True, but I'll bet the Grand Canyon Hotel will be an adventure."

"Adventure is not the word I would have chosen," Bob said.

I had no idea how right my prediction would turn out to be.

We pulled into Williams about 2:30 p.m. It took forever to get everyone picked up at their respective homes. Sidney forgot his laptop computer, and we had to go back to his home to retrieve it. Sidney without his laptop was like a day without sunshine. A train was going through Williams when we arrived.

We waited for the train to pass, so that we could cross the tracks to the hotel at 145 W. Route 66. I read from a guidebook, "Williams was the last town to fight against the closing of Route 66. There were court cases and it dragged on for years. In 1984, I40 opened, and, after assurances that there would be at least three exits for Williams from I40, the fight was dropped and, one year later in 1985, historic Route 66 was decommissioned."

Rest in Peace, Route 66

Historic Grand Canyon Hotel in Williams, Arizona

"The town in Coconino County is named for William 'Old Bill' Williams, a mountain man and trader. It's 43.8 square miles and the 2006 census reported 3,094 people, up from 2,842 in 2000."

"Where is the hotel?" asked Bob, as the train finally cleared the street.

"Right there!" I pointed to a small building that definitely looked like something out of the 1800's. We parked the car right in front and approached the hotel's front door. Although we could see inside, the door to the hotel was locked.

"Are you sure this place is still even open?" asked Bob.

"Yes, I'm sure. I reserved two rooms for us here," I answered.

We were just preparing to get back in our car when the door opened and Amy, the hotel proprietor, beckoned. "I'm sorry. I was just cleaning the rooms. We don't officially open for check-in until three p.m. That's when I open the front door. I clean the rooms before then. But it's almost three p.m. now." She smiled.

The four of us trooped inside, and Amy told us the rules of the house. "You can go upstairs and pick any room that has its door open. That means it isn't rented. There's only one bathroom on each floor, though. There are no televisions, but there is a computer room with Internet service down here."

With this, Amy beckoned towards a door off the small cramped lobby. I thought I heard Sidney breathe an audible sigh of relief.

We went upstairs and soon discovered that only two rooms were available. Both were brown and gloomy.

"This is going to be some interesting night, I think," said Bob.

"Agreed," said Shelly.

As we went back downstairs to get our things from the car, Amy said, "There's a walking ghost tour tonight of the area downtown known as Saloon Row. I highly recommend it---especially the Red Garter Bed & Bakery, which is at 137 West Railroad Avenue."

"What's so interesting about a bakery?" I asked.

Amy looked uncomfortable. "It hasn't always been a bakery. A German tailor named August Tetzlaff in 1897 built it. It had a saloon on the first floor and other businesses that operated in the building."

Amy continued, somewhat uncomfortably, "There used to be a flight of steps on the side of the building nicknamed the Cowboys' Endurance Test. The cowboys would climb to visit the 'soiled doves' in the upper reaches of the bar where the girls plied their trade. For years, Longino Mora operated the saloon. He also sold liquor during Prohibition. He was a fascinating pioneer man who was born in 1848 at the end of the Mexican-American War. He worked for the U.S. Cavalry, taking freight to Army posts out in the desert and he was a scout who chased Geronimo and Cochise through the Arizona Territory and Mexico. He was married five times and had twenty-five children."

"Wow!" Bob exclaimed. "Twenty-five children! All local gals?"

" All his wives came from Mexico," said Amy. " Two died of cholera. Two died in childbirth. Clara, his last wife, was fifty years younger than Longino. They had their last child when Longino was eighty. Of course, prostitution was banned in Arizona in 1907, but enforcement was spotty. However, when it was still going on, one of the upstairs girls stabbed a customer in the back. He fell downstairs and tumbled right out the front door, dying in the street. That probably had a lot to do with the enforcement of the 1907 blue law becoming stricter."

Shelly looked lost in thought. "That Longino guy must have been something!"

We all agreed with her.

Since we had heard that the Red Garter was converted to a barbecue restaurant in 1984 and we were all getting hungry, we decided to wander over and see if we could scrounge up something to eat. (The answer: no. Now it's a bakery and there are no ribs for sale.)

We spent some time talking to the Red Garter owner who bought the building in 1979. He remodeled the eight former brothel rooms into four expansive guest rooms with a Western Victorian flavor. He changed the downstairs from a restaurant to a bakery, so our hopes for barbecue were dashed. Not to worry, there was a place with a green awning that had good food nearby.

When we had finished, we agreed that we would prefer to break out the traveling ouija board and some other games in our small, dark rooms, instead of paying what seemed a rather exorbitant price of over twelve dollars per head for the walking tour. We had already wandered over to the Williams Depot, which is kitty-corner from the hotel and located inside a former Fray Marcos Hotel built in 1908. Fred Harvey's "Harvey Girls," young women who were paid well and received free room and board, staffed the hotel. They wore uniforms consisting of a black dress that fell to just above the ankle and a crisp white apron.

Mary Tobin, the clerk at the Williams Depot for five years, claimed to have seen a young Harvey Girl floating three feet off the ground by the back door, close to the ticket counter. A second girl, dressed similarly, the ticket agent was able to identify from old photos in the museum as being Clara, a four foot eleven inch spitfire who, she said, likes to throw shirts around in the gift shop and performs other pranks. (If you want to see for yourself, you will need to visit 233 N. Grand Canyon Blvd.)

By now, we all felt we had done a pretty good job on our own of seeing the small town, without paying over twelve dollars to find out about "ghosts we have known and loved." We returned to our hotel rooms to play one of the board games we had brought, although not the Ouija board. Shelly said that the room we were sharing was so creepy she didn't want to risk it.

When Shelly and I entered our room to get the games, the door slammed shut behind us. It took us a while to pry the door back open. It seemed to be locked from the outside. We thought the boys were playing a joke on us. That was not the case. The boys were waiting downstairs, in the combined game room/computer room, which was roomier and would allow us to gather in one spot. There would be no drinking, however. The hotel makes you buy your booze from them and drink it in your room…something about the liquor license.

At around midnight, after numerous trains had passed through the town making a great racket, we all decided to turn in.

Shelly and I would share the brighter of the two rooms. Sidney and Bob would be in what Shelly had dubbed "Haunted Hollow." It was a pretty creep-looking old room, and the blankets and linens in each room were very dated. Everything was as though it had been there since the hey-day of the Red Garter down the street.

We walked the boys to their room and Sidney dropped to one knee and said, "Hey! Look at this! Someone's socks are under my bed."

"Actually, Sidney, it's *our* bed. I thought we'd at least have two single beds," said Bob. He didn't look happy about sharing a bed with Sidney, given the fact that the beds of that era were very small.

"Hey! What do you expect for fifty-nine dollars a night?" I asked. "And don't forget that Amy said there's free coffee downstairs in the morning. We can grab some baked goods from the Red Garter and head on to our next town along Route 66."

"And what town is that, oh Mighty Guide Girl?" asked Bob sarcastically.

"Seligman," I replied. "Seligman, Arizona."

Historic Route 66 and Interstate 40, as well as the Southwest Chief Amtrack Route intersect in Williams, Arizona, the last town along Route 66 to give up fighting the closing of the Mother Road. The Southern terminus of the Grand Canyon Railroad is actually three miles east of Williams, and the town is 60 miles south of the Grand Canyon itself.

The brighter and cheerier of the two rooms, which Shelly and I occupied. Note the antique decor of the furniture, mirror and pictures. In the night, it felt as though someone perched themselves on the foot of this bed. In the morning, when we investigated, a slight indentation could be seen where someone or something had been sitting. As we entered, a young lady was just finishing turning down the coverlet, but it appeared that she left no reflection in the mirror. Perhaps the mirror was tilted, we thought. Later, in speaking with Amy, we learned that the hotel employs no other maid staff, as only Amy and her husband, Ken, run it.

"Haunted Hollow," as Shelly dubbed the gloomy hotel room Bob and Sidney shared. The door does not lead to a bathroom, as there is only one bathroom on each floor, which all rooms on the corridor share. In the night, one of the two pictures seen to the left of the door fell to the ground, shattering the glass. None of us got a good night's sleep.

The Spirits of Seligman

The next morning when Shelly and I emerged from our dreary room in the Grand Canyon Hotel in Williams, we were a bit the worse for lack of sleep.

"Did you guys hear those trains going through town every thirty minutes? No wonder Amy asked if we wanted earplugs," I said to Bob and Sidney, as we gathered in the lobby, lugging our suitcases down unaided, since there was no elevator.

"I didn't care about the trains. Sidney snores louder than any train. But it had to be at least eighty-five degrees in our room. We had no window and no air conditioner. The ceiling fan wasn't cutting it." Bob, too, looked as though he had slept poorly in the Grand Canyon Hotel. "I feel like I've been rode hard and put away wet."

"At least you didn't have someone come sit on the foot of your bed in the middle of the night," Shelly said. She looked genuinely upset.

"Who or what sat on your bed?" asked Sidney.

"A young Hispanic woman in a white dress." Shelly seemed quite convinced.

"Are you kidding?" Bob asked.

"No. I'm not kidding...but I'm not sure if I was awake or if I was dreaming, either. The only thing that makes me think it was real is that in the morning there was an impression in the brown bedspread at the foot of our bed as though someone had been sitting there. I don't remember that from when we checked in."

"And how about that maid thing?" I said. I proceeded to tell the boys about the nonexistent maid Shelly and I had encountered cleaning our room.

"Do you remember John Holst at the Red Garter telling us that people say they see that apparition? Some call her Eve, but others think it's Clara, the last wife of that old geezer who got married five times." This was Sidney's contribution. I was surprised Sidney hadn't remembered "that old geezer's" name, which was Longino Mora. Sidney must really be rattled if he wasn't remembering every detail of everything in his usual efficient fashion. He was the trivia king.

"How did you sleep, Sidney?" I asked.

"Awful! I had the feeling all night that someone was staring at me. Then, about two o'clock in the morning, a picture fell off the wall and broke. Neither one of us were anywhere near it."

"You know what it's supposed to mean when a picture falls off the wall like that, don't you?" asked Shelly. "It means that someone died in that room!"

"I'm just glad it wasn't me," muttered Bob. "Sidney snores like a steam engine and he passes gas in the night."

Everybody laughed except Sidney.

"Well, " I said, ignoring the flatulence remark, "on a brighter note, we're off to Seligman. Have you all had your morning coffee? It's free."

"We've been down here for a while," said Sidney. "It might be free coffee, but I would advise against drinking it." He cocked an eyebrow to indicate that the coffee was less-than-satisfactory in his eyes.

"All right-y then," I said, as cheerily as I could muster under the circumstances. "Who's up first for driving to Seligman?"

There was no lack of takers. We set off with Bob behind the wheel.

Display on Main Street in Seligman, Arizona

I began reading to the other three in the car from a Legends of America website I had run a copy of, trying to play Sidney for once, and inform everyone about our next stop, Seligman, Arizona.

"Listen up, ladies and germs, here is what that website had to say about Seligman: "Seligman, Arizona is a Route 66 town all the way. This delightful town retains all the flavor of the old road."

Bob interrupted me, grumpily, "I'll be the judge of that delightful crack."

I continued, " A trip down Route 66 in Seligman is a trip back in time to the days when Route 66 was the Main Street of America. Founded in 1895 after the completion of the Peavine Railroad, the railroad camp known as Prescott Junction officially became Seligman and was an important railroad stop along the line. Seligman embraced Route 66 wholeheartedly upon its arrival in the late 1920's. The railroad and tourist traffic from Route 66 became Seligman's main source of economic security. In the late 1970's Seligman was bypassed by the Interstate, and the Santa Fe Railroad ceased its operations in the town in 1985. Many old towns with similar histories would have faded away once they were bypassed, but not Seligman."

"Well, I guess we'll see about that," said Bob. "So far, not so delightful. I about sweat to death, somebody died in our hotel room and left his socks under the bed, and you girls had a ghostly visitor who sat on the foot of your bed. Or so says Shelly.

We were pulling into Seligman, which looked like a circus had driven through and left its cast-off props on the sides of its main street. I continued reading:

A typical abandoned hotel along Route 66

"Between 1889-1891, Seligman was established by the Theut and Moultrie families. They were prosperous slaughterhouse owners in Southern antebellum families who lost everything in the Civil War and the following Reconstruction periods. They moved West hoping to find a new life in the largely uninhabited territory of Arizona and took over the area of Seligman Campsite from the Cherokee Indians."

Seligman, Arizona

"Eeeuuuwww," said Shelly from the back seat. "Slaughterhouse owners? And they stole this place from the Indians?"

We were now in the middle of beautiful downtown Seligman. All I could think of to say was, "Why would anyone want to steal this place from anybody else?" Seligman looked pretty junky, to me.

Sidney corrected me. "Laura, that's not fair. I'm sure it was a beautiful sight during the days when the Cherokee Indians roamed the plains. It's just that all this stuff has ruined its natural beauty."

In front of a building known as Seligman Sundries, old cars were sitting, allowing visitors to have their picture taken with various cutouts of famous people from the fifties. There were two old Edsels, decrepit in the extreme, parked on main street. Kitty-corner from the Sundries store was a bar called The Black Cat, which I had heard was haunted. We pulled into its gravel parking lot.

I had called ahead and spoken to a famous citizen of the town named Juan Delgadillo, a man who had done more than anyone to build up the Route 66 network. Knowing we'd arrive about lunchtime, I arranged for Juan to fill us in on the strange doings inside the Black Cat after dark. The Black Cat was not his business, however. He had founded the Snow Cap Drive-In in 1953, building it from leftover boards and materials. Angel, who was the town barber, and his brother Juan Delgadillo had worked hard to try to keep the town alive. Both said that when Route 66 stopped being the main drag, the town died instantly. Today, only 456 people live in Seligman.

We trooped into the Black Cat, which was dark and smelled musty. It was easy to imagine someone getting knifed in a bar fight here on a Saturday night.

A woman bartender was mopping the bar with a rag.

"Is Juan Delgadillo here?" I asked.

"You must mean John or Robert Delgadillo."

"No. I'm quite sure the man I spoke with on the phone said his name was Juan."

"Honey, John Delgadillo is sitting over there, in his usual spot, eating lunch. Ask him about Juan."

The four of us trooped over and introduced ourselves to the pleasant-looking stranger. "Are you Juan?" I asked.

"No. Juan was my father," the young man said.

" I talked to Juan on the phone about interviewing him for a possible article for our school paper, the *Lumberjack*." I knew that this was the first Shelly and Bob and Sidney had heard of this plan of mine to write up our adventures. "We all attend Northern Arizona University in Flagstaff," I explained.

"When I spoke with Juan, he said he would fill me in on the haunted places in town, and he especially mentioned this bar, which is where we agreed to meet."

John smiled.

"It's entirely possible that the Black Cat is haunted. If it is, and my father said to meet him here today, the person haunting it may well *be* my father, Jose Delgadillo. Dad died June 2 of 2004."

"Yikes!" said Shelly.

I sat down. Hard.

"Can I buy you guys a drink?" asked John.

"Yes, please, and make it a strong one," I said. I was still reeling in shock from John's disclosure. Obviously, it was not just name confusion between Jose and John, or John would have known about my call.

So who was that on the phone last week?

I made an executive decision, "We're going to keep on keeping on, Troops. We are NOT going to be staying in Seligman for the night. Onward to Kingman. And, having finished our drinks, we left.

A typical Route 66 roadside business, now that the Mother Road has bypassed the towns along the route.

When we passed this home-lettered sign along the Route 66 highway, it set off many jokes about our accommodations, so far. "Do you have us booked in that motel, Laura?" asked Bob, with a grin. "And, if you do, don't forget that Shelly prefers a bathtub."

Kingman, Arizona

Kingman, Arizona looks like a big city when you come directly from Seligman, with its fewer-than-500 inhabitants. It has 27, 271 residents and, when you factor in the surrounding area, it becomes a thriving metropolis of 40,000.

The town, founded in 1883, is named for Lewis Kingman who supervised the building of the railroad from Winslow to Beale's Spring. There's also an interesting bit of history involving Lieutenant Edward Fitzgerald Beale, a naval officer who was hired by the government to build a wagon road and to test camels to see if they would be good mounts in the desert climate.

We had been taking turns driving for hours, and we were tired. The hotel of choice for this town was the Hotel Brunswick at 315 East Andy Devine Road (928-718-1800).

I'd become a little leery of reading too much about ghosts of the places we were supposed to stay. I suppose I was still a bit shell-shocked by the revelation that I had talked to a dead man in Seligman on the phone. I decided to fill the group in on the amenities of the next hotel.

Bob asked, "What's this next place like? I hope it's not a dump."

Laughing about the sign we had seen along the road, Shelly said, "I hope it's not the Bates Motel!"

I ignored them all and continued.

"No, this place has always had a reputation for quality. It has cable TV, air conditioning, the Internet, a restaurant, a bar, Amtrak transfers, complimentary continental breakfast, accepts pets, has a laundry and dry-cleaning service and also has a library, a business center and a sitting room."

"Sounds like a step up from our previous digs," observed Bob wryly. "Sidney shook his head in agreement.

"The Internet room at the Grand Canyon looked like it was really a storage room. All the tables for the computers were too low to be comfortable," Sidney commented. If Sidney would notice anything, it would be the computer amenities.

"How big is this place?" Shelly asked.

"Well, now it's twenty-four guest rooms and suites and nineteen have private baths in them," I replied.

"Let's make sure we get two rooms with bathrooms," Shelly said. "Running down the hall to a shared bathroom is definitely not my cup of tea. And I'd like one with a tub, not just a shower."

"Oh, darn!" I said, smiling. "I'll have to cancel us out of the Bates Motel, then. And I hear it's got a great taxidermy collection in the lobby, too!"

Bob remained silent for a minute. Then he said, "Just how old *IS* this place?"

"The hotel was built in 1909, but it earned a reputation for elegance right from the start. It used Waterford crystal, brass beds, and there was a telephone in every room, back when that was unusual," I said.

"Wow! Waterford crystal goes for about $60 a glass. My mom has some. Kildare, I think is the pattern she has." Shelly said.

"Right, Shelly, but who needs a land line when we all have Sprint cell phones?" Bob held his up as he spoke. "What else? What aren't you telling us?" asked Bob.

"Well…there are reports of ghosts in three of the rooms. Especially in room 202. One ghost is a man, one is a young girl, and I don't know what the third one is."

"Why is this male ghost hanging around?" asked Sidney. "Usually, there's a reason for a spectral presence."

On the road

"Perhaps you'll understand better if I just read you this excerpt from the March 13, 1915 *Kingman Daily Miner*: "W.D. McCright was found dead in his room at the Brunswick Hotel last Sunday morning, death coming without warning. He had evidently arisen at the usual hour and was making his morning absolutions when the grim terror called. Not making his appearance at the usual hour, Mr. Miller went to his room and found Mr. McCright, a wealthy businessman, lying on the floor, dead, with a towel in his hands. Mr. McCright was seventy-three."

The group said nothing for a few minutes, and then Sidney said, "Let's make sure we don't get *that* room."

Nervous laughter.

"What does that mean--- 'the grim terror'?" asked Shelly.

Bob said, "That's just old-fashioned speak for death. Old obituaries used to be quite interesting. Nowadays you're lucky if you can figure out what the poor guy died from."

"So, what room number did McCright meet the Grim Terror in?" asked Sidney.

"That would be room number 212, according to the obituary," I said, " but we might want to opt out of room 202, as well."

"Why?" asked Shelly. "What happened in 202?"

"I'm not sure we know, but that's the one that has a little girl haunting it, and the third ghost, gender unknown, roams around and is very particular about the placement of a footstool of some kind."

"Great," said Bob under his breath. "Now we have to worry about the exact placement of furniture."

"The history of the hotel is kind of interesting," I continued. "Want to hear it?"

"Sure," said Bob and Sidney simultaneously. Bob added, "We might as well know what the Grim Terror might have in store for us if we stay in this joint."

"It seems that this hotel, when built, was the first three-story building in Kingman. Three years after two guys named Thompson and Mulligan teamed up to build the hotel, they both fell in love with the same woman, Sarah, who chose to become Mrs. Mulligan. Since the two partners were now at odds and caught up in this love triangle, they decided to built a partition down the middle of the hotel and split it into two separate hotels. Mr. Thompson ended up with twenty-five rooms and the restaurant. Mulligan got twenty-five rooms, the girl, and the bar."

"Sounds about right," observed Bob. "He got the girl and he needed to start drinking heavily."

"Bob!" Shelly said, laughing. "That's not very nice. He was probably very happy being married to Sarah. After all, he won out in wooing her over his ex-partner."

"Well, Shelly," I said. "He might have been happy that he got the girl, but she died only a few years later of a chronic condition, so his happiness was short-lived. They think that one of the ghosts haunting the hotel is Sarah's. I figure she's the one who is so particular about the placement of that footstool. After all, it *was* her home."

So, we don't want to be put in 202 or 212. Any other rooms to avoid?" asked Sidney.

"The current owner, a Frenchman named Gerard J. Guedon, says that there was some minor trouble in 201 when a German couple stayed there and a ghost tried to pull the wife out of bed."

"I hate when that happens," said Shelly. "Just like in that movie 'Paranormal'!" Everyone laughed. "Also, Mr. Guedon, himself, has had some experiences in room 312 that involved yellow magic marker."

"Yellow magic marker?" said Sidney.

"Yes. Something about coming downstairs in the morning and having a yellow mark on his neck. Then, his girlfriend came downstairs and she had a yellow mark on her neck, too."

"I'll bet it wasn't marker," said Bob, smiling.

"Mr. Guedon says he has tried to make peace with the ghosts of the Brunswick, and he feels that there's a truce. He says that it cost him almost twice as much as he anticipated to remodel the place. One night when he had been venting out loud to himself about the cost overruns, he noticed that pennies kept appearing on the bar in the morning. Every night, the bar would be cleared off. Every morning pennies would appear. Some said they saw a small child leaving a trail of pennies in the hallway. Gerard believes this was a sign of helpfulness on the part of the ghosts and a signal from them to him that his financial prospects were going to improve, which they did."

Sidney, always the realist, said, "Did he check the dates on those pennies?"

"I don't know. Why?" I asked.

"They were probably rare coins...Indianheads or something. He might have checked." Leave it to Sidney to think of the one thing that others forgot.

We arrived at the hotel at 315 E. Andy Devine and it looked shabby chic like all the other old hotels we'd seen. It really resembled, more than anything, those old saloons you see in old movie sets, with a railing above, from which the gunslingers often fell after being shot.

"I'm not impressed," said Bob. "Isn't there somewhere else we can stay?"

"Well, there is one other hotel I scoped out, but you're not going to like it."

"Why not?" asked Bob, the practical one.

"I heard about this place from some kids at a Sonic Drive-In."

"Yesssss," Sidney said in a completely serious tone of voice. "I usually get my lodging tips from children hanging around Sonic drive-ins." He rolled his eyes.

"Oh, stop that! I was just talking to these kids because they said they were passing through Flagstaff from Kingman, and one of them told me that there was a sadistic dentist who used to take

some of his female patients, in whom he had more than a professional interest…"

"Is it safe to say he was looking at more than their teeth?" Bob inquired, also with deadpan seriousness.

"It is safe to say that he took a series of young, female patrons to this motel, killed them and cut them up."

Shelly looked slightly ill as this tid-bit sank in. "Where is this place?" she asked.

"Well, that's the thing," I said. "The boys didn't know the exact address. They said the hotel was called the Beale Hotel and was on Main Street, but I wasn't able to find an exact location. Also, one boy said the guy was a doctor and one guy said he was a dentist, so that was unclear."

"So, there are more hotels on this Main Street?" asked Shelly. "And we should try to stay healthy so we don't need to consult either dentists or doctors while here."

" If we can find the street there are more motels. I think there was even an incident involving a movie star who came and posed topless outside one of them. The City Fathers made her apologize, in person."

"You mean there's a chance that we won't find the one motel where some maniac went to cut up his patients?" asked Bob.

"Well, these were teen-agers. Although I'm sure there is some basis in fact for what they were telling me, they didn't seem too well-informed."

"Let's take a vote," said Bob. "How many want to find Main Street and some modern motel or hotel that may or may not have harbored a homicidal maniac?"

Three hands went up.

"How many want to go stay in the Hotel Brunswick, where every other room is definitely haunted?" asked Bob.

I reluctantly raised my hand. Outvoted, three to one.

"There is one other thing you should know."

"What's that?" asked Sidney.

"There was a horrible catastrophe on July 5, 1973 in Kingman when some firefighters were transferring propane from a tanker to a storage tank. There was an explosion that killed eleven firefighters. It's called a BLEVE."

"What's that mean?" asked Shelly.

"Boiling Liquid Expanding Vapor Explosion," responded Sidney.

"Right again, Sidney. I guess you probably know about the twenty-four cubic feet of data on this event that is stored in the Arizona State Archives. Firefighters use the catastrophe to study and make sure nothing like that happens again. There have been some stories of firefighters who were killed in the explosion haunting the site."

"Is the site anywhere near that street with the new motels, where the doctor or dentist may or may not have taken his women victims?

"No. I don't think the storage tanks were anywhere near the motels along Andy Devine Avenue, which is sort of Main Street,

"Anyone in here watch that television series 'Prison Break'?" asked Bob.

"I did," I said. "I really liked it, especially season one."

"Well, if I remember correctly, Lincoln Burrow's son was sent to some reformatory or something in Kingman, Arizona, for a while, and then released."

"That's right!" I said. "I remember that episode. And I remember a 'Sopranos' episode where Tony gets shot and thinks he has exchanged identities with some insurance salesman from Kingman, Arizona. And there's a Steve Zahn movie with Jennifer Aniston called 'Management' where his family owns a motel in

Kingman. Not a very snazzy one. Probably a lot like the one we'll be staying in, though."

"Well, I still vote for the new motels along Andy Devine Avenue. Keep your eyes open for Pamela Anderson. As far as I'm concerned, she'd be a welcome sight after what we experienced last night. With any luck, our choice of motels won't put us in the very same room with the mad doctor or dentist."

And so we headed towards Andy Devine Avenue to look for a new motel for the night.

You never know what you'll see along Route 66.

The Oatman Hotel, Oatman, Arizona

Oatman, Arizona

We wanted to stop in Oatman because of the wild burros that come into town each day to be fed. Supposedly, these burros are the descendants of the burros that miners used back when prospecting for gold. When the burros were no longer useful in mining the gold found in the area as early as 1902, they were turned loose. These wild animals are their descendants.

"So, we're going there to see a bunch of donkeys?" Sidney asked. "Or are they called asses?"

I just gave each of them a look that conveyed my secret thought about their unfortunate use of that term.

"Well, we're going there for the donkeys and to learn about another Route 66 town. They have Route 66 signs and memorabilia all over the place. I'm interested in the origins of the town's name," I said.

"Start at the beginning, Laura," pleaded Shelly.

"Okay, from my research---which includes some conflicting reports---I've determined that the town was founded in either 1905 or 1906. In 1915, two miners made a $10 million dollar gold strike and the town's population quickly mushroomed to 3,500 people

within a year. There isn't much indication that it ever got that much bigger, although one website did claim it grew even more.

One of the big attractions of the town is the honeymoon suite where Clark Gable and Carole Lombard stayed, at the Oatman Hotel, after their marriage on March 18, 1939. There are some reports that Gable used to return to Oatman to play poker with the locals, too. But the most fascinating part of the town's history, to me, was the way it got its name. Originally named Vivian, it was named after a young girl of thirteen or fourteen from Illinois, Olive Oatman, who was traveling west with her father, Royce Oatman, his wife and their seven children. Rebellious Apache Indians attacked them and killed the entire family except for Olive and her younger sister Mary Ann, then aged seven. A brother, Lorenzo, who was sixteen or seventeen at the time, was thrown from a cliff and presumed dead, but he also survived.

Olive was traded to the less-rebellious Mohave Indians and eventually ransomed by someone named Quechan for a horse, four blankets and some beads."

"Wow," said Shelly. "It would be tough to have a price on your head like that and know exactly how much someone else thought you were worth. You guys would probably ransom me for a Hershey bar and a Pez dispenser."

I continued, "Olive had been held captive by the Mohave Indians for five years and ten days. She returned to Fort Yuma to be reunited with her brother, Lorenzo, on February 28, 1856. Olive hit the lecture circuit after her release from captivity and explained that she and her sister Mary Ann, who died while a captive, were immediately tattooed, which was a sign that they were slaves of the tribe, not a marking signifying marriage. In fact, Olive, while on the lecture circuit, is said to have commented, 'To the honor of these savages, they never offered the least unchaste abuse of me.'

"She sounds kind of disappointed," Bob observed wryly.

"Yet there persists on websites a legend that a son named John convinced the townsfolk of Vivian to rename the small village Oatman in her honor. On the other hand, some say Olive never had a son.

The Oatman Hotel, which was built in 1902, in addition to serving as Gable and Lombard's honeymoon suite (room 15), and has been featured in at least three movies, including 'How the West Was Won,' "Foxfire,' and 'The Edge of Eternity.'

Most of the town burnt down in 1921, and United Eastern Mines shut down their operations in 1924. Nineteen twenty-four was also the year that the hotel had to be rebuilt after a fire swept through the town. At the time, it was a two-story adobe building called the Durlin Hotel. Its Mission Spanish Revival architecture makes the hotel significant. It's been listed on the National Register of Historic Buildings since 1983.

On the walls and ceilings of the bar and restaurant are dollar bills signed and dated by miners who were in Oatman hoping to strike it rich. Anna Eder, the operator of the hotel back then under the name the Eder Café, allowed men to post the marked bills against what they owed."

"Sounds like a funny way to run a business," said Bob.

"You would say that," responded Shelly, "being a business major."

"So, where are we going to stay," asked Sidney, "and why do I already know what you're going to say?"

"Yes, we have reservations at the Oatman Hotel, but, alas, not in room fifteen."

"What ghosts will we have to watch out for?" asked Shelly.

"Well, the most famous one was the town drunk who died behind the hotel of acute alcohol intoxication and was not found for two days. Legend has it that he was buried where he was found in the alley. He's supposed to be a bit of a prankster, a sort of poltergeist, and is called 'Oatie' by the locals."

"What was his real name?" Sidney asked.

"His real name was William Ray Flour. He was a boarder in the hotel. He was an Irishman who was trying to strike it rich in the gold mines so he could bring his wife and two children across the ocean to reunite as a family. His family never made it to America. All three family members perished during the voyage, which probably didn't help William's drinking problem. He died, cold and alone, in 1930 in the alley behind the hotel."

"Wow! Way to lighten our mood," said Shelly.

"So, what's the address of this hotel we're staying at?" asked Bob.

"181 Main Street, Route 66, Oatman. (928-768-4408.)"

"We'll compare notes in the morning on Oatie's antics," said Shelly, with a smile. "He's not supposed to be dangerous, is he?"

"Far from it, Shelly. And he's supposed to like women better than men, so good luck to you two," I said to Bob and Sidney as we headed off down the hall to our own room.

Dinosaurs...or replicas of them...along Route 66.

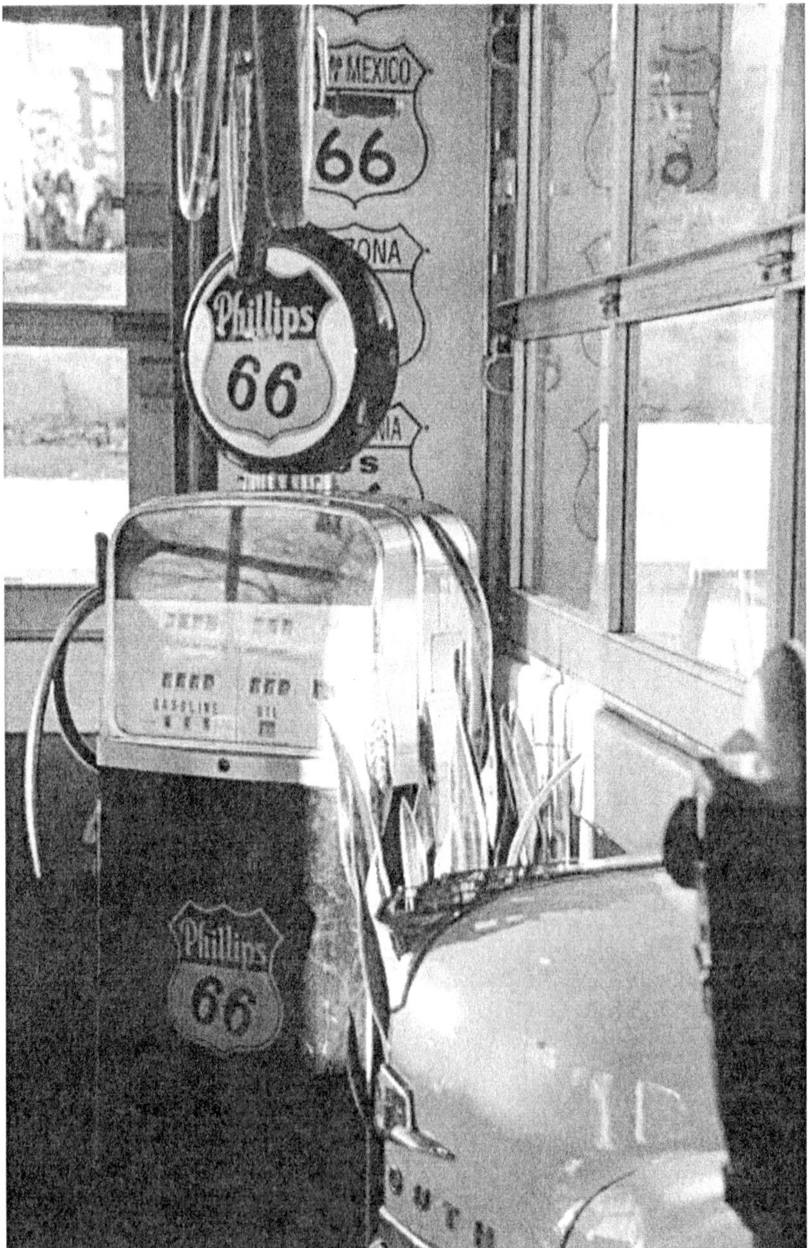
66
Phillips
66
Phillips
66

"Go West, Young Man!"

In the morning, after our stay in Oatman, no one had experienced the fabled two a.m. bagpipe serenade from "Oatie," the poltergeist ghost of the Oatman Hotel. We were ready to cross the border into California.

"California, here we come!" Bob said, with fake bravado. We all laughed.

"Where, exactly, are we going in California?" asked Sidney. A reasonable question.

"Well, all I know, for sure, is that we will hit Bastow and Santa Monica Pier, where the road ends. I think there's even a one-hundred-year celebration of the pier, complete with fireworks, which we might catch, if we're lucky. After that, we have some choices. Which would you lot rather do: visit San Bernadino looking for ghosts, or go to West Hollywood and the Sunset Strip?"

Relic of the past along Route 66.

Speaking simultaneously, all three said, "Sunset Strip."

Why did this not surprise me?

"Okay. I hear you. But we are definitely going to visit Barstow first. There's a historic Harvey House that has been turned into a Route 66 Museum, and they have a neat bridge that leads to the train station, which goes right by it."

"How do you know so much about it?" asked Sidney, who seemed miffed that his position as Mr. Know-It-All of 1999 was being usurped.

"Well, after all, it *was* my idea to take this road trip, and I feel a certain obligation to try to pick cities and hotels and places that we will remember fondly later on."

'Fondly...is that the correct adjective?" Bob asked, with a grin.

"So, it's onward to Barstow, then," said Shelly.

To which Sidney responded, "To infinity and beyond!"

The original Casa del Desierto Harvey House, now the Route 66 Museum in Barstow, California.

"Okay, kids," I said to the yawning quartet that greeted me in the morning in Barstow's Motel Six, "today's big adventure will take place at the historic Casa del Desierto, which was a a rail depot and restaurant, back in the day.

"What day?" asked Bob.

"Judging from the year it was built, which was 1911, any time from then on. Now, it's the Route 66 Museum."

Deborah Hodgkin met us in the basement of the historic Harvey Hotel at 681 N. First Avenue. We had approached the museum across a bridge similar to the Old Chain of Rocks Bridge in St.Louis which has a turn in it, so that you can see the entire railway below.

Route 66 Museum at 681 N. First Avenue.

In the old days, people alighted from the trains and stayed in the Harvey House Hotel. There was even a 1946 movie starring Judy Garland that romanticized the Harvey House female employees, girls who had to take a vow not to marry while employed by the Harvey House and had certain other morals clauses in their work agreements.

We watched a movie, narrated by Marty Milner of "Route 66" television fame, that tracked the Mother Road (so named by John Steinbeck in "The Grapes of Wrath") all the way from Chicago to California, with Milner at the wheel of a classic Chevrolet Corvette.

The Casa del Desierto boasted a rail depot, restaurant and hotel complex and is listed on the National Register of Historic Places. The original alignment of Route 66 was in front of this building **between the railroad tracks. Route 55, itself, was made from the National Old Trails Road, which crossed the Mojave Desert.**

As the boys examined several of the trains parked on the siding outside the building, I spoke with Deborah.

"Have there been any ghosts associated with this building?" I asked.

"As a matter of fact, yes, there have. There is a story that a Harvey House girl found herself pregnant by her boyfriend, who ran out on her.

Casa del Desierto, Barstow, California

She fell---or jumped---- under one of the approaching trains, and no one thinks it was accidental. Since that time, many who visit the gift shop or the hotel have reported seeing a young woman wearing a long black skirt, and crisp white blouse and apron, who seems to linger on the upper terrace of the old hotel. When they approach, she disappears. They say she looks very sad."

"Does anyone know what her name is?" asked Shelly.

"Not really. The locals call her Julia."

"If we hung around here tonight, is it possible we would see Julia?" asked Sidney.

"All things are possible, Kids, " said Deb, "but there are no guarantees in life."

"No kidding. That poor girl must have been really upset about her boyfriend running out on her like that, in her condition, especially since Harvey House girls signed affidavits saying they wouldn't marry while they were working at the Harvey House," said Shelly.

"Well, teachers in the old days used to have to do pretty much the same thing," said Shelly, whose mother had been a teacher for many years. My grandmother started teaching in 1927 and she had to quit when she got married."

"Wow! Times have sure changed," said Bob. "Now, your biggest worry is that the teachers will marry the students!"

"Oh, Bob, don't be stupid," I said. "That doesn't happen often."

"Often enough," Bob said with a wink.

"Are there any other haunted Route 66 icons in the area you could point out? " I asked Deborah.

"There's an El Rancho restaurant that is pretty strange," said Ms. Hodgkin. "You might want to check that out. And we've had a few leapers."

"Leapers?" I repeated.

"You know…people who leap from the bridge. Suicides. But if you really want to visit a bridge that has had more than its share of suicides and has become haunted, as a result, you need to go visit Suicide Bridge near Pasadena."

As we headed out to find the El Rancho Restaurant and start our drive to Suicide Bridge, we left a contribution.

The Museum was founded in 2000 and charges no admission, but accepts donations. Volunteers staff the Historic Harvey House and the museum hosts special exhibits and upcoming events, including a Miss Route 66 pageant, a Route 66 Quilt Show, Artists & Authors and Desert Writers' Day and group tours of the facility. Students attending Barstow Community College may also apply for the Barstow Route 66 Mother Road Museum scholarship, designed to bring more awareness to Main Street, USA. It is open from 10 to 4 p.m. on Fridays and Saturdays, and from 11 to 4 p.m. on Sunday afternoons.

Soon, our drive around town yielded a run-down structure, which bore the sign El Rancho Restaurant. Since we were all hungry, we went in.

Each of us ordered a burger, and then we voted.

"So, next stop, Suicide Bridge?" I asked.

"Yes, but after that, you have to promise that we get to go through West Hollywood and the Sunset Strip at night, when they have all these impersonators," said Sidney.

"Sidney, you aren't planning on wearing your Star Wars Storm trooper gear, are you?" laughed Bob.

Sidney looked insulted. "If I were going to be anyone from that movie, I'd go as Luke Skywalker, " he said.

"Not me," said Bob. "I'd want to be Darth Vader. He was the one with the real power."

"Oh, I see. A power freak in our midst. That explains so much, Bob," I smiled. "Let's get going, then, so we can make it to Suicide Bridge. I hear there's a steady stream of jumpers throwing themselves onto the rocks below."

"Great," said Shelly, with a grim look. "Just what I was hoping to experience on this trip."

"Hey…. I aim to please." I picked up the check and headed toward the cash register.

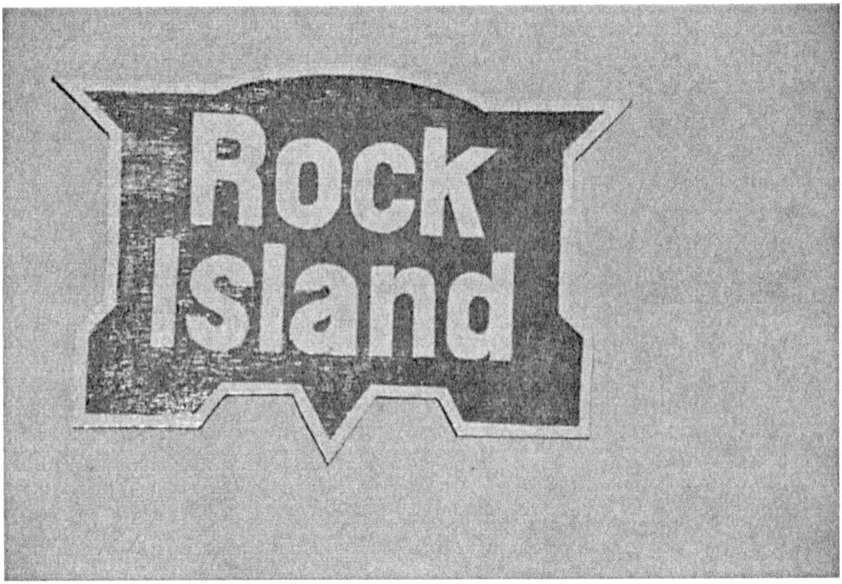
Rock
Island

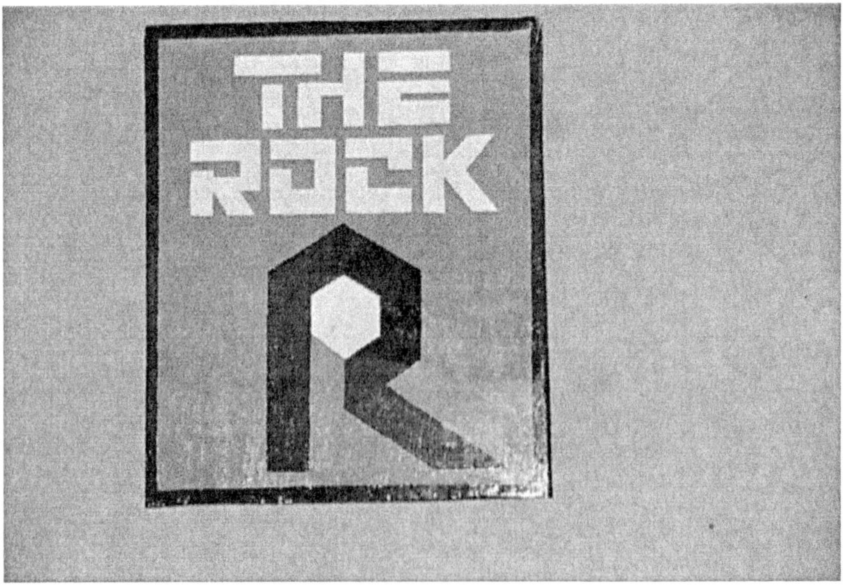
THE
ROCK

El Rancho Barstow

Route 66 Restaurant in Barstow, California.

128

Trains outside the Barstow, California Route 66 Museum.

Suicide Bridge, Pasadena, California

"Tell us about this bridge we're heading for, Laura," said Shelly.

"Well, it was built in 1913 as the Colorado Street Bridge, named after the main east-west drag of Pasadena. It stands 150 feet tall and is 1,467 feet long, stretching across the Arroyo Seco. The canyon links the San Gabriel Mountains to the Los Angeles River. It used to really be hard to get there, before this bridge was built. Some call it the Arroyo Seco Bridge because of the Arroyo Seco Stream that runs beneath it, but that's not really its name. And it quit being part of Route 66 in 1940, when the Arroyo Seco Parkway opened."

Shelly piped up. "I've read about this place. There's supposed to be a lot of paranormal activity near Devils Gate at the top of Lake Avenue in Altadena."

"I didn't know you were in to paranormal societies," I said.

"Actually, I just read up on some of it for this trip," she responded. "We have to go out there at three a.m. That's when the paranormal investigators say the vibes are the strongest."

"Oh, is that so, Mrs. Ghost Expert?" I said with sarcasm.

"Yes, that's what I read online."

"Shelly, if you read it online, it must be true," Sidney said, and I didn't detect any sarcasm in his support of her plan for us to visit the bridge at three a.m.

"So tell us of the ghosts, Mrs. Ghost Expert," I continued.

"Well, there are, of course, many ghosts, as some workers were killed while the bridge was under construction way back in 1913. The J.A.L. Woddell Firm of Kansas City, Missouri supervised, and the Beaux Arts arches and ornate lampposts and railings and the curve were courtesy of John Drake Mercereau, who was the engineer on the project. One poor guy is supposed to have fallen headfirst into the wet cement from a great height and was buried right in the bridge."

"Wow. Talk about your migraine headaches!" said Bob.

"There are those who insist more than just that one man died while building the thing. All of the men who died while the bridge was under construction are supposed to haunt the place."

"What about the leapers?" I asked.

"The first one was on November 16, 1919. Then, it just got worse and worse, especially during the Great Depression. On January 21, 1937, 'Time' magazine reported that a nineteen-year-old girl had become the eighty-ninth person to commit suicide by jumping off the bridge, so the City Fathers finally erected a seventy-one foot steel fence to stop people from jumping. It cost $7,000. It didn't stop the leapers, though. One of the most bizarre was a young woman who threw her baby over the side four months later, on May 1, 1937, and then leaped to join the child. However, the child's blanket caught in some tree branches and the baby lived. The mother was not so fortunate. In one year they had more than fifty suicides. Overall, there have been more than one hundred deaths by suicide, steel fence or no steel fence."

"Reminds me of a documentary I saw on the Golden Gate Bridge," said Bob. "They get about two or three leapers a month."

"So, what do the hauntings consist of...so we know what to look for at three o'clock in the morning?"

"I know what I'LL be looking for, " Bob said," a nice soft bed."

"No, Bob. We've come all this way and we're going to do this right. If Shelly says that three a.m. is the best time to catch ghostly activity, we're all going to come out here this morning and see for ourselves," said Sidney.

And that is exactly what we did.

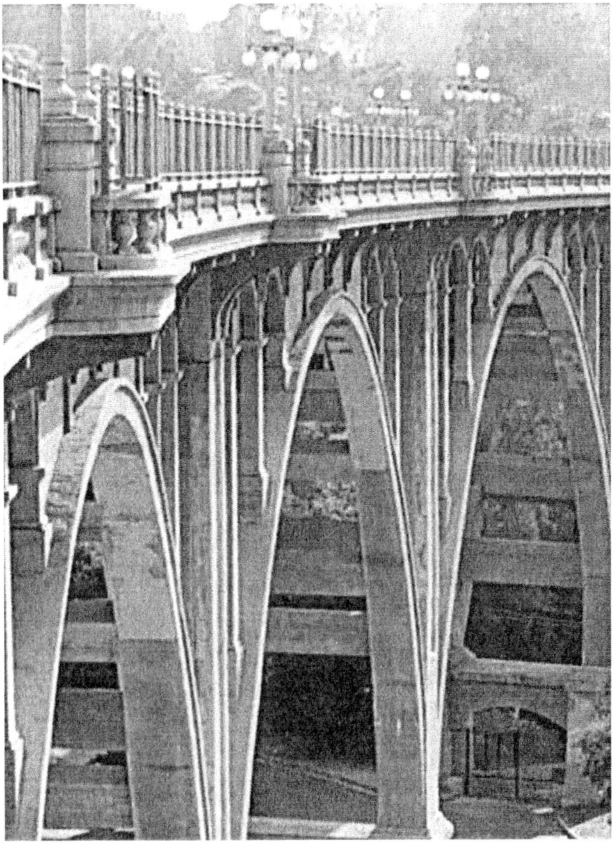

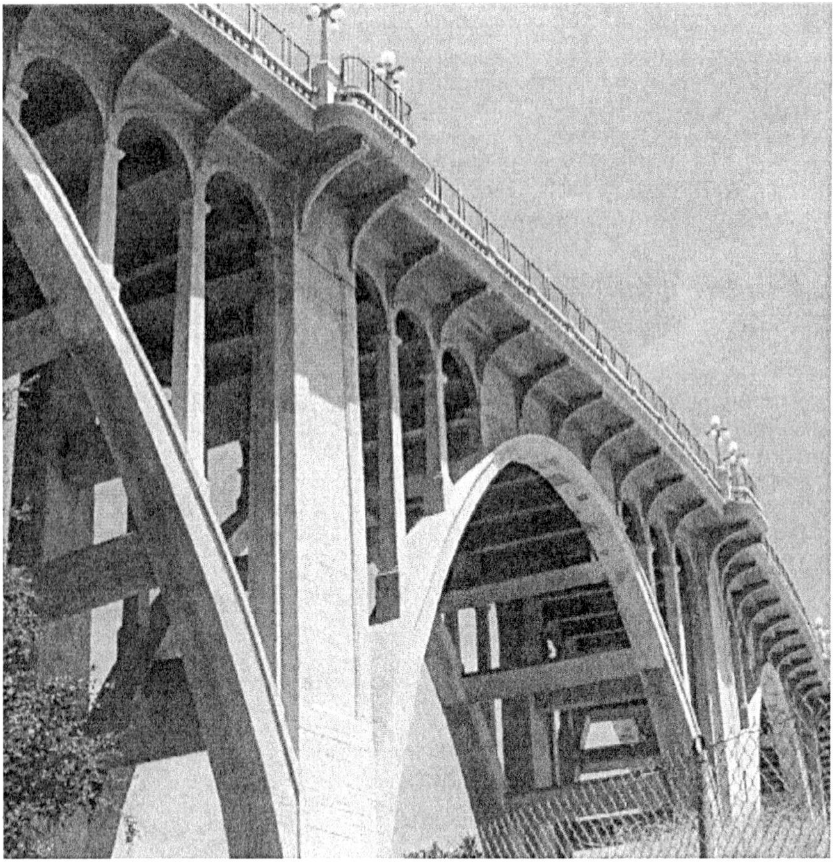

The first sign of trouble was a man wearing wire-rimmed glasses, who seemed to be dressed in a very old-fashioned manner. None of us had read the article that Shelly had, which described this fellow as hurrying across the bridge, apparently in search of something.

Another commonly sighted ghost was a woman who appears on the parapets that appear periodically along the perimeter of the structure. She is dressed in long flowing robes and leaps before anyone can stop her.

Then there is the mother who threw her child over the edge of the bridge. She is apparently searching for the child in death.

All we saw was a really odd sight, a man dressed as a clown. This was not what we had expected to see, and none of us, at first, could quite believe it. He looked odd in broad daylight, let alone at three o'clock in the morning.

Bob smiled at me and said, "Now there's somethin' you don't see ever' day." We both laughed, even though there were other paranormal investigators on the bridge, and we felt as though we were the amateurs amongst professionals. None of us saw any leaping ladies or flying babies, but the clown was definitely on the bridge.

"That is just WRONG!" said Sidney.

"What?" we asked, in unison.

"A clown. Near the bridge. There is nothing scarier than a clown, and to have one appear on Suicide Bridge…well, let's get out of here," Sidney said. And he didn't seem to be kidding.

We left, feeling somewhat sheepish that we had not sighted any ghosts on Suicide Bridge, but, for what it's worth, the bridge does have a very "heavy" feeling at three o'clock in the morning. But that may have just been us, as we were all so tired we could barely function. We went back to our Holiday Inn and slept till checkout time.

Tomorrow, we would gas up the '57 Chevy and head for home, four from Flagstaff who had had some extraordinary adventures, even if our final stop wasn't one of them.

And who knows what else we might do on our summer vacations of the future?

GHOSTS OF INTERSTATE 90 Chicago to Boston   by D. Latham

GHOSTS of the Whitewater Valley by Chuck Grimes

GHOSTS of Interstate 74   by B. Carlson

GHOSTS of the Ohio Lakeshore Counties   by Karen Waltemire

GHOSTS of Interstate 65   by Joanna Foreman

GHOSTS of Interstate 25 by Bruce Carlson

GHOSTS of the Smoky Mountains by Larry Hillhouse

GHOSTS of the Illinois Canal System by David Youngquist

GHOSTS of the Niagara River by Bruce Carlson

Ghosts of Little Bavaria   by Kishe Wallace

Shown above (at 85% of actual size) are the spines of other Quixote Press books of ghost stories. These are available at the retailer from whom this book was procured, or from our office at 1-800-571-2665 cost is $9.95 + $3.50 S/H.

Ghosts of Interstate 75	by Bruce Carlson
Ghosts of Lake Michigan	by Ophelia Julien
Ghosts of I-10	by C. J. Mouser
GHOSTS OF INTERSTATE 55	by Bruce Carlson
Ghosts of US - 13, Wisconsin Dells to Superior	by Bruce Carlson
Ghosts of I-80	David youngquist
Ghosts of Interstate 95	by Bruce Carlson
Ghosts of US 550	by Richard DeVore
Ghosts of Erie Canal	by Tony Gerst
Ghosts of the Ohio River	by Bruce Carlson
Ghosts of Warren County	by Various Writers
Ghosts of I-71 Louisville, KY to Cleveland, OH	by Bruce Carlson

GHOSTS of Lookout Mountain by Larry Hillhouse	
GHOSTS of Interstate 77 by Bruce Carlson	
GHOSTS of Interstate 94 by B. Carlson	
GHOSTS of MICHIGAN'S U. P. by Chris Shanley-Dillman	
GHOSTS of the FOX RIVER VALLEY by D. Latham	
GHOSTS ALONG I-35 by *B. Carlson*	
Ghostly Tales of Lake Huron **by Roger H. Meyer**	
Ghost Stories by Kids, for Kids by some really great fifth graders	
Ghosts of Door County Wisconsin by Geri Rider	
Ghosts of the Ozarks *B Carlson*	
Ghosts of US - 63 by Bruce Carlson	
Ghostly Tales of Lake Erie by Jo Lela Pope Kimber	

GHOSTS OF DALLAS COUNTY by Lori Pielak
Ghosts of US - 66 from Chicgo to Oklahoma By McCarty & Wilson
Ghosts of the Appalachian Trail by Dr. Tirstan Perry
Ghosts of I-70 by B. Carlson
Ghosts of the Thousand Islands by Larry Hillhouse
Ghosts of US - 23 in Michigan by B. Carlson
Ghosts of Lake Superior by Enid Cleaves
GHOSTS OF THE IOWA GREAT LAKES by Bruce Carlson
Ghosts of the Amana Colonies by Lori Erickson
Ghosts of Lee County, Iowa by Bruce Carlson
The Best of the Mississippi River Ghosts by Bruce Carlson
Ghosts of Polk County Iowa by Tom Welch

Ghosts of Ohio's Lake Erie shores & Islands Vacationland by B. Carlson
Ghosts of Des Moines County   by Bruce Carlson
Ghosts of the Wabash River   by Bruce Carlson
Ghosts of Michigan's US 127   by Bruce Carlson
GHOSTS OF I-79   ***BY BRUCE CARLSON***
Ghosts of US-66 from Ft. Smith to Flagstaff   by Connie Wilson
Ghosts of US 6 in Pennslyvania   by Bruce Carlson
Ghosts of the Lower Missouri   by Marcia Schwartz
Ghosts of the Tennessee River in Tennessee   by Bruce Carlson
Ghosts of the Tennessee River in Alabama
Ghosts of Michigan's US 12 by R. Rademacher & B. Carlson
Ghosts of the Upper Savannah River from Augusta to Lake Hartwell   by Bruce Carlson
Mysteries of the Lake of the Ozarks   Hean & Sugar Hardin